for Sofía and Lucio

Text and illustrations copyright © 2016 by Pamela Prichett
Cover and book design by 40N47 Design, Inc.

All rights reserved.
CIP data is available.
Published in the United States 2016 by
🍎 Blue Apple Books
515 Valley Street
Maplewood, NJ 07040
www.blueapplebooks.com
First edition 7/16
Printed in China
ISBN: 978-1-60905-528-8

Downward Dog with Diego

Pamela Prichett

BLUE  APPLE

I'm learning yoga.

Do you want to learn, too?

Just follow the animals...

and do what they do!

STRETCH

like a Cat...

...jumping in

a **bog.**

...get as low as

a **log.**

BALANCE

like a Bear...

Lie Down

like a **Crocodile**...

...make it

a **habit.**

STAND

like a Cow...

FLUTTER

like a **Butterfly...**

...touch your heels

to your **thighs.**

Now, just be **YOU**...

...and do what you **do!**

special thanks to my yoga teacher Kamila Faruki

the animal poses (and their funny* names)

cat
marjariasana
- stretches and strengthens the back, neck and shoulders (pairs with cow)
- relieves stress and calms the mind

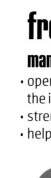

frog
mandukasana
- opens up the hips and stretches the inner thighs
- strengthens the lower back
- helps the digestive system

cow
bitilasana
- stretches and strengthens the back, neck and shoulders (pairs with cat)
- massages the tummy
- improves circulation in the chest

rabbit
sasangasana
- relieves tension in the neck, shoulders and back
- refreshes the brain, reduces tiredness, aids sleep

downward facing dog
adho mukha svanasana
- strengthens the hands, wrists, shoulders, back, calves, hamstrings, and achilles tendons
- energizes the body

*asana is the sanskrit word for pose

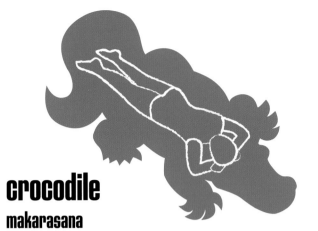

crocodile
makarasana
- relieves muscle fatigue after other poses
- relaxes the body and mind

lion
simhasana
- relaxes and strengthens the muscles in the face and throat
- relieves tension in the chest
- keeps the eyes healthy

balancing bear
merudandasana
- opens up the hips and stretches the back of the legs
- strengthens the tummy and tones the inner organs
- improves balance and concentration

cobra
bhujangasana
- stretches the shoulders, spine and abdominal muscles
- opens the chest and invigorates the heart

butterfly
purna titali asana
- relaxes and stretches the thighs
- opens up the hips and improves flexibility
- relieves stress and tiredness